Let's Have a Sleepover

By Bonnie Lasser
Illustrated by S.I. Artist

g A GOLDEN BOOK · NEW YORK

Golden Books Publishing Company, Inc., New York, New York 10106

Dear Barbie,

The other night I slept over at my friend Jessica's house. It was my first sleepover. I wanted to go, but once I got there I was frightened. Suddenly all I wanted to do was go back home. I didn't tell Jessica how I felt because I was afraid she might laugh at me. But now I'm worried about the next time I have a sleepover. How can I keep from being afraid?

Did this ever happen to you?

Love,
Tanya

Barbie sat down to answer Tanya's letter. She wrote:

Dear Tanya,
  Your letter makes me think of the time my little sister Stacie and her friend Emily had a sleepover at our house. They had fun, but Emily got a little homesick.

Here is the story Barbie told. . . .

One Thursday afternoon, Stacie and Emily chatted
excitedly as they walked home from school.

"I can't wait for you to sleep over tomorrow night,"
said Stacie. "We're going to have so much fun!"

"Are you excited about spending the night at Stacie's?" asked Emily's dad at dinner that night.

"Yes, but I'm not sure what to bring," said Emily.

"I'll help you pack after we clean up," offered Mom. "I went to a lot of sleepovers when I was your age."

"Don't forget your toothbrush," said Mom as she and Emily washed the dinner dishes.

"Will Stacie think I'm a baby if I bring my teddy bear?" asked Emily.

"I don't think so," said Mom. "Take it if you want to."

"See you tomorrow," Emily said as she waved goodbye to her parents the next morning. But as she said it, she suddenly felt scared. Tomorrow seemed so far away!

Later that day, Stacie and Emily walked hand-in-hand to Stacie's house.

"You'll get to meet my new dog, Ginger!" said Stacie excitedly.

"I can't wait!" said Emily, and for a moment she forgot that she was scared.

When the girls got to Stacie's house, Barbie was outside playing fetch with Ginger. The minute Emily saw them she began to miss her own dog, Murphy. But she didn't say anything.

"Let's show Emily where to put her bag," said Barbie, heading for Stacie's bedroom.

Suddenly Barbie noticed that Emily didn't look very happy.

"Is everything okay, Emily?" asked Barbie.

"Well, I . . . I guess so," said Emily. "It's just that I miss my family."

"That's perfectly natural," said Barbie, and she put
her arm around Emily.

"I'm just not used to being away from them," said
Emily. "I keep wondering if they're okay."

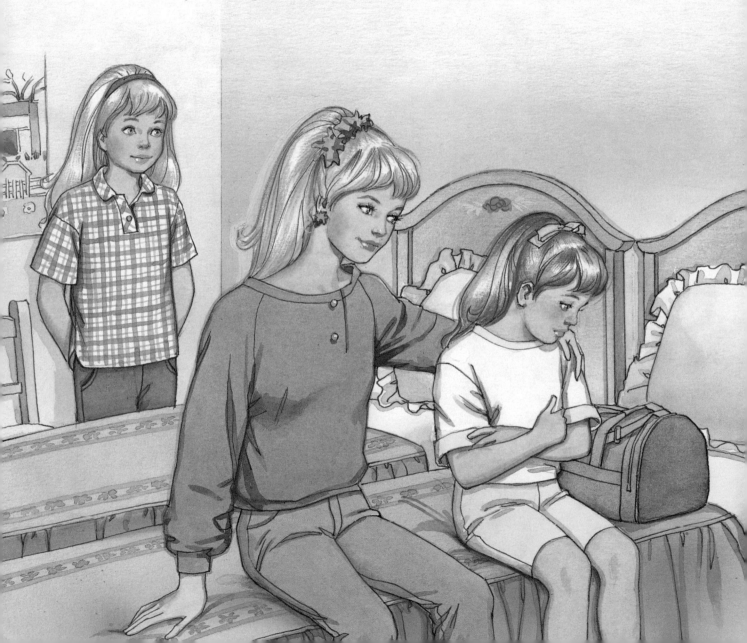

"I'm sure they're fine," said Barbie, "but maybe you'd like to talk to them."

"I'd love to!" said Emily, and her face brightened.

After Emily called home, she felt much better. The homesick feeling began to go away.

After dinner, Barbie had a surprise for the girls.

"I rented Stacie's favorite movie and made popcorn," she said.

"Great!" shouted the girls as they raced to the TV room.

"I can't believe it! This is my favorite movie, too!" Emily exclaimed.

After the movie, the girls got ready for bed.

Emily noticed that Stacie was hugging her teddy bear, so she happily unpacked hers.

Then Barbie tucked the girls in and wished them sweet dreams.

Suddenly Emily heard a strange noise. "What's that?" she asked.

"That was only the wind," Barbie answered. "I'll keep the hall light on, and I'll be in the next room if you need anything."

That made Emily feel much better, and she soon fell fast asleep.

For breakfast the next morning, Barbie made the best silver dollar pancakes Emily had ever had!

"Stacie, thanks for having me over," said Emily. "Next time you can sleep at *my* house."

"That would be great!" said Stacie. Then she paused and looked up at Barbie. "And I'll call *you* if *I* get homesick, okay?"

"Of course," said Barbie, smiling.

Barbie finished her letter to Tanya:

At sleepovers you might get a little homesick at first, but that's okay. That feeling usually goes away after awhile. And don't forget that, if you feel like it, you can always call home!

Love,
Barbie